Merry Christmas 2008

To
Karter Kotz

From
Matt & Jenn Picinich

for Leah, Abe, and Benny,
the coolest of the cool

Published by Hallmark Books,
a division of Hallmark Cards, Inc., Kansas City, MO 64141

Editorial Director: Todd Hafer
Editor: Theresa Trinder
Art Director: Kevin Swanson
Designer: Mary Eakin
Production Artist: Dan Horton

ISBN: 978-1-59530-016-4
BOK6094

Printed and bound in China.

GIFT BOOKS
from Hallmark

Rodney
Reindeer
and the Holiday HATastrophe!

by Tom Shay-Zapien
Illustrated by Ivan Chan
& Ralanna Forbis

Tickety-tock! Tockety-tick!

The hands of the Countdown Clock were slowly and steadily winding down, and all around the North Pole everyone was doing something or going somewhere. There was so much work to do!

It was the hurriest, flurriest time of year. And no one was more excited about it than Rodney.

He skip-hopped through the sparkling snow
all the way to Santa's garage.

"How's the sleigh, Santa?" asked Rodney.
"Do you need any help waxing it? Shining it?
Washing it? Drying it?"

"We're just about done, Rodney. All I've got
to do now is take it for a little test drive.
Say, would you like to . . . ?"

But before Santa could even twitch a whisker, Rodney was sitting in the passenger seat of the shiny red sleigh, ready to ride.

"Yahoo!" shouted Rodney, as they zipped and zoomed over the Pole. "Can you do any tricks?"

"Nothing fancy this time," said Santa. "Just a quick flight check."

"Aw, come on, Santa," pleaded Rodney. "Couldn't we do just one little loop-the-loop? Please?"

"Well . . . okay, Rodney," Santa said with a grin. "But just one."

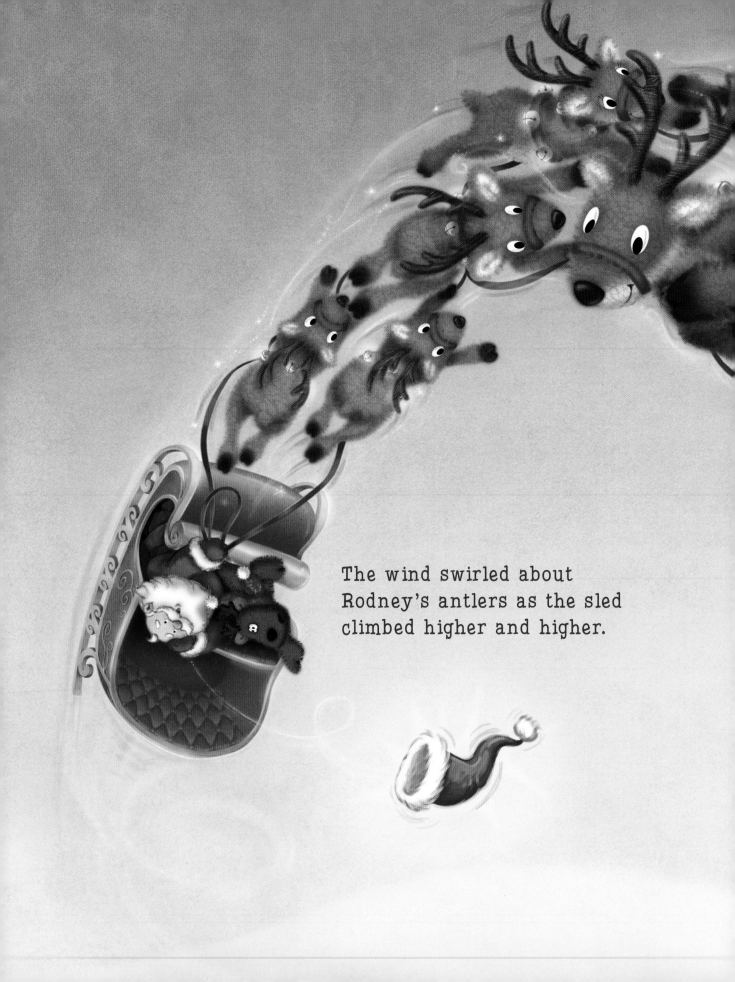

The wind swirled about
Rodney's antlers as the sled
climbed higher and higher.

And as he hung upside down, a tickle
of excitement danced around in his belly.
All he could see was sky! And then . . .
a quick flash of red.

Santa's hat! It blew right off of his head
and twirled away. And away. And away.

"Santa! What are we going to do? I don't see it anywhere!" Rodney gasped.

"We've got to find that hat," Santa said nervously. "It's the only hat I've ever worn on Christmas Eve. Mrs. Claus made it just for me. And my head gets so chilly!"

"I'm sorry, Santa," said Rodney in a small voice. Boy, did he feel terrible. None of this would've ever happened if he hadn't begged Santa for all that fancy flying.

By Christmas Eve morning, the news had spread
all across the Pole. Search teams had come up
empty-handed. Gloom blanketed what had always
been the most magical day of the year. And no one
had ever seen Santa so unjolly.

Rodney sat in the square and looked around
the sad little town.

He thought. He thought some more. And then
he had an idea.

"Santa! Rodney! Any word?" Rhonda asked
hopefully. "Has anyone found it?"

"Not yet," said Rodney. "But I think you can help!"

Rhonda nodded as Rodney explained his plan.
In no time at all, elves were rushing to and fro
with hatboxes of all shapes and sizes, trying
desperately to help Santa find something he liked.

He tried them all.

Chef hats!

Clown hats!

Cowboy and crown hats!

Hats for sailing!

Hats for siestas!

Hats made of fruit!

Hats for fiestas!

"Oh, who am I kidding?" Santa sighed. "Can you
imagine me shimmying down the chimney in
THIS? It's no use. I could never replace my old hat."

Everyone in the shop got very silent. "It's hopeless.
Simply ho-ho-hopeless!"

SNOWMAN'S LAND

NORTH POLE

HAWAII

It was clear to Rodney that his idea wasn't going to work. He just had to find that hat!

So he combed through the powdery drifts they'd flown over just a few days before. And after hours and hours of searching, he glanced over at the horizon, where the sun was just starting to set.

And suddenly . . . could it be? He thought he saw it! So he set off over the biggest hill in town to the chilliest place in the North and South Poles combined.

Snowman's Land.

It WAS Santa's hat . . . on top of
the scariest, scowliest, grouchiest,
growliest snowman Rodney had
ever seen.

Mr. Blizzard! An eyeful of frightful!
And he towered over Rodney like
an avalanche.

"Ahem, ex-c-c-cuse me," stuttered Rodney. "I see you've f-f-found Santa's lost h-h-hat."

"Lost? This hat's not lost at all!" bellowed Mr. Blizzard. "Why, it was delivered to my door only yesterday. By AIR mail, in fact! And just in time for Christmas."

Rodney wanted that hat so badly, but he didn't know what to do.

"Now go on home," grumbled Mr. Blizzard. "Before I lose my cool!"

So Rodney went back to Rhonda's hat shop. In fact, he ran there, never looking back. Not even once.

"Santa! Santa! I found your hat!" he called. "But the surliest, burliest old snowman found it first!"

"Hmm . . . I think I know just the snowman you're talking about," said Santa.

And from inside his fuzzy coat pocket, he pulled out a long yellowed scroll. Rodney knew he had seen that before. It was the OFFICIAL LIST— the who's who of good boys and girls all around the world.

"Just as I thought," said Santa with a smile. "Mr. Blizzard. One winter hat."

Rhonda shuffled through the back room and emerged with a beautiful cap in the merriest shade of green. "I've been saving this one for a special occasion," she said.

And just to make it extra special, Mrs. Claus expertly knitted a big red B onto the front.

She and Rhonda and several elves helped wrap it all up with shiny paper and curling ribbon in the fanciest hatbox they could find.

"Okay, Rodney!" called Santa. "Time for our first delivery!"

"Who's there? What's all that racket? Who dares disturb . . . "

Mr. Blizzard was lost for words when he saw Santa Claus. THE Santa Claus. At HIS door.

"A present for you, Mr. B! Merry Christmas!"

"A present? But I didn't . . . I wasn't . . ."
stammered Mr. Blizzard. "I haven't . . .
been very good this year."

"Don't be silly," said Santa. "Everyone deserves
a do-over!"

"Open it! Open it!" Rodney cheered. As he peeled
away the wrap, Mr. Blizzard could hardly believe
his eyes. It was exactly what he wanted.

Mr. Blizzard placed the hat on his head and
tied the strings. He handed the red hat with
the furry trim to Santa. Santa handed his cap
to Rodney. And they hiked back to town together
through the twirling, swirling snow without
feeling the slightest breeze.

They made it back just in time for take-off.
Santa puckered his cherry nose. His cheeks
started to get a little rosy. His belly even shook
a bit as he laughed.

"Ho ho ho! Merry Christmas!"

And as Santa flew up, up, up, and out of sight,
he was as jolly as ever.

Hat's off to YOU!
We'd love to know if you've enjoyed this book.

Please mail us a letter:
Book Feedback
Mail Drop 215
2501 McGee Street
Kansas City, MO 64108

Or e-mail: booknotes@hallmark.com